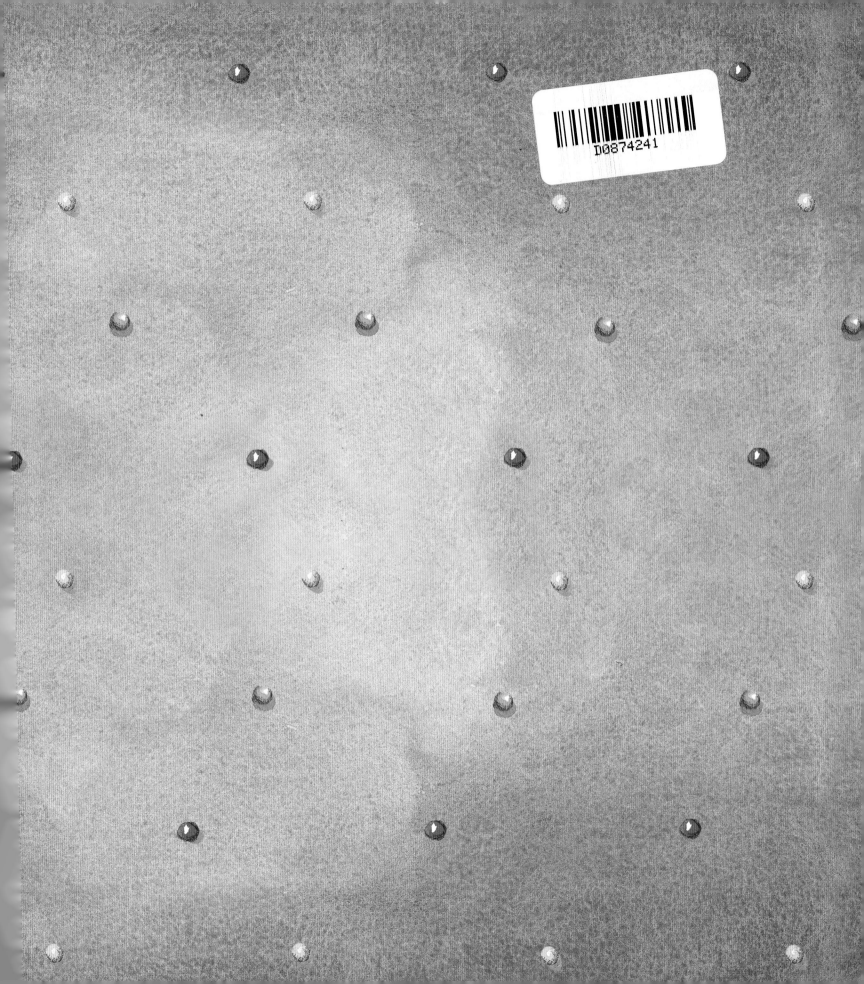

For Liz Flanagan with thanks - SG

For Joe, Lily and Gabriel, and Tiziana as ever - JB-B

A PAVILION CHILDREN'S BOOK

First published in Great Britain in 2003 by
Chrysalis Children's Books
The Chrysalis Building
Bramley Road
London W10 6SP
www.chrysalisbooks.co.uk

Designed by Sarah Goodwin and Keren-Orr Greenfeld

A CIP catalogue record for this book is available
from the British Library.

ISBN 1 84365 026 6

Printed in China by Imago

2 4 6 8 10 9 7 5 3 1

This book can be ordered direct from the publisher. Please contact
the Marketing Department. But try your bookshop first.

ARCHIE'S AMAZING ADVENTURE

Sally Grindley
Illustrated by John Bendall-Brunello

Chrysalis Children's Books

Early one evening, something happened at the animal park.
Archie the giraffe was trying to reach a delicious-looking leaf
when he leaned against a gate – and it opened!
Archie couldn't believe his eyes. "An open gate means an animal
could get out!" he thought. Then he realized, "An open gate means
I could get out!"

So out Archie went.

Nobody saw Archie tiptoe along the grassy path.

Nobody saw him **slither** down the muddy bank.

Nobody saw him wriggle through the prickly hedge.

Somebody saw him **leap** out onto the road, but it was too late.

Archie was off and away.

Archie jogged and skipped and galloped along the road.
"I'm free," he chortled, "look at me."

Then two flashing lights dazzled him, a blaring horn deafened him, and he had to jump for his life –

"Yikes!"

He landed in a ditch.

"Ouch!" came a small voice from somewhere underneath him.
Archie unscrambled his legs and a head popped up.
"What on earth are you?" it asked.

"I'm Archie, the giraffe," said Archie. "What are you?"

"A rat, of course! I'm Totty, and I'm big for my age, but you're enormous."

"Giraffes are," Archie nodded importantly. "I'm on an adventure."

"I'm coming, too," squealed Totty.

So off they went.

Soon, Archie and Totty saw colourful lights ahead, and then they heard music.

Sometimes at the animal park, Archie's keeper played music and Archie adored it.

"Yippee!" he cheered.

He bounded round a corner and they found themselves at the edge of a fairground.

"Wow!"
said Totty.

She'd never seen anything like it.

Crowds of people were bobbing up and down on carousels, screeching round on bumper cars, hurling balls at coconuts and smothering their faces with candyfloss.

"Come on, Totty," said Archie. "Let's go for a ride!"
He leapt onto a bumper car and put his foot on the accelerator.

"Hold tight!" he yelled.

"Beep beep," squealed Totty,

as they hurtled round and round.

Next they climbed aboard the Ghost Train.

"Who turned the lights out?" cried Archie as it chugged into the tunnel.

"I don't like the dark!" shrieked Totty, hiding under Archie's ears.

When they saw Archie's shadow, the children on the Ghost Train screamed even louder. "There's a dinosaur! We saw a dinosaur!"

Archie staggered out into the daylight and suddenly realized how hungry he was. A little girl standing close by was eating candyfloss.

Archie stuck out his tongue and tasted it. "Ugh!" he spluttered.
"It's like eating cobwebs."
"Delicious," said Totty, grabbing a piece for herself.

Then Archie smelled a smell that made his mouth water. He charged over to a burger bar. Before anyone could stop him, he emptied a whole bowl. "Onions," he smiled. "My favourite."
"Ugh!" said Totty.

Crowds of people were following Archie now.
Some were friendly, some were shouting at him,
some were pointing at Totty and screaming,
and children kept pulling Archie's tail.

"Quick, Totty," he said. "Let's get away." He galloped towards
the Big Wheel. As he clambered aboard, it began to turn.
"Where are we going, Archie?" squeaked Totty.

Up and up they went.
"I'm scared," wailed Totty.
"I can see the animal park,"
shouted Archie. "I can
see my mum!"
"I want my mum," cried Totty.

Round and down they went.
Then up and up again.

Round and down they went once more.

They were just nearing the bottom when Archie spotted a group of men with a huge net.

"Time to go home, I think," he said.

"Get ready to jump, Totty."

The Big Wheel slowed and Archie leapt to the ground.

The men with the net ran at him, but Archie made a dash for it ...

... he ran through the crowds,

past the burger bar,

BURGER BAR

DODGEMS

past the dodgems,

Carlo's CAROUSEL

past the Helter Skelter,

past the carousel,

and away!

It was night time now, but as Archie and Totty walked back along the road, the moon shone brightly.

"That was fun," said Totty.

"Wasn't it?" said Archie.

"Can I come with you on your next adventure?" asked Totty.

"Of course you can," said Archie.

Then the two friends said goodbye. Totty jumped back in her ditch, where her mum was looking out for her. Archie found the gate and slipped back through, just in time for bed.

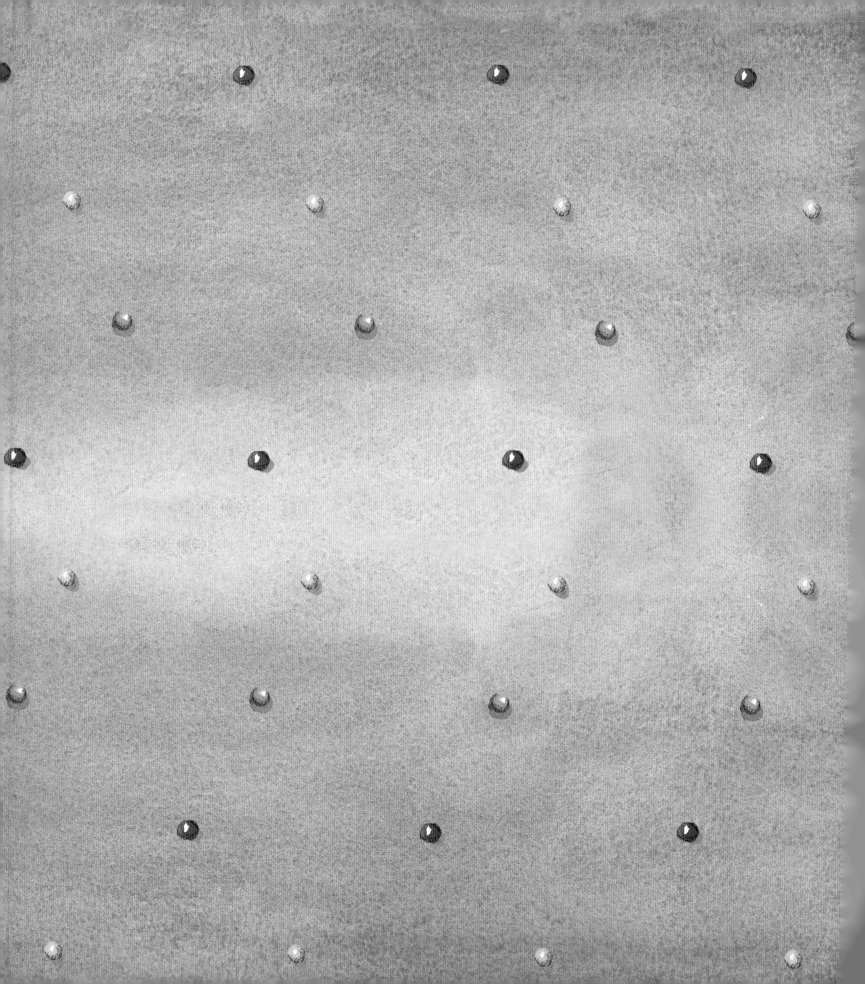